The Little Girl and the Bear

Retold by James Riordan

Illustrated by Alex Ayliffe

Chapter 1

Once upon a time there was a little girl
who lived in a cottage next to a big
forest. One day the little girl said to
her mother and father, 'Please may
I go and play in the forest?'
'Yes,' they said, 'but don't go too
far away.'
So the little girl ran off to play in
the forest.

First she ran along the path and then she jumped over a log. It was a hot day and soon she was tired, so she sat down on the grass. She looked all around and then decided to pick some of the beautiful flowers.

The little girl went deeper and deeper into the dark forest. She was so happy picking flowers that she forgot to watch where she was going. Suddenly she found that she was lost.

'Help! Help!' she shouted, but she had gone so far into the forest that no one could hear her.

Just then the little girl heard a sound behind her. As she turned round she saw a big brown bear. When he saw the little girl, the bear smiled.

'Ah, my little one,' he said. 'I have been looking for someone to do my housework. You must come home with me.'

The bear pulled the little girl by the arm and led her off to his house.

When they came to the bear's house,
the bear told the little girl all the
things she had to do.
'Clean the floor, make my bed, chop
wood for the fire and cook my dinner,
or I will eat you.'
The little girl was very unhappy.

She didn't want to work for the bear,
but she didn't know how to find her
way home and she was scared that
the bear would eat her.

So day after day the little girl
cleaned and cooked for the bear.

But she never stopped thinking about
how she might find her way home.

Then one day she said to the bear,
'I want to take some cakes to my mother
and father to show them that I am well.'
'No, no, no!' shouted the bear. 'I am not
stupid. You will not come back.'
But the little girl asked him again and
again until the bear said, 'I will take the
cakes to your mother and father myself
in the morning.'
This is just what the little girl had hoped
he would say.

So the little girl made lots of cakes.
'I will put the cakes in this basket,' she
said to the bear. 'And when you set out
I will climb on to the roof and watch
you all the way.'
'Yes, yes,' said the bear.

As soon as the bear was asleep, the little
girl climbed on to the roof of the house
and made a cross from some wood. She
put her hat, coat and scarf over the cross.

Then the little
girl climbed into
the basket and
hid under the dish
of cakes.

Chapter 2

When the bear woke up he saw the
basket of cakes, put it on his back,
and set off through the forest.
It was a warm day and the basket
was very heavy. Soon the bear was hot
and tired, so he sat down under a tree.
He was just about to open the basket
and eat one of the cakes when he heard,
'Don't eat the cakes!'

'That sounds like the little girl,' said the
bear. He looked back at the house.
He could see the little girl on the roof.
'My, my, what big
eyes she has got,'
he said and he
went on his way.

On and on the
bear walked.
Then it began
to rain.

'I'll just stop under this tree and eat
a cake,' he said. 'The little girl can't
see me now. I'm too far away.'
But as soon as he sat down he heard,
'Don't eat the cakes. I can see you.'

The bear looked back at the house.

He could just see the little girl on the roof.

'My, my, what big
eyes she has got,'
he said and he
went on his way.

Chapter 3

At last the bear came out of the
forest. He walked down the road
and came to the little girl's cottage.
He opened the gate, went up the path,
and put down the basket of cakes.
'Is anyone at home?' he shouted. 'I have
some cakes for you. They are from
your little girl.'

When the dogs in the village heard the bear shouting, they came running to chase him away. The bear ran as fast as he could back into the forest. He was very cross.

'When I get home that little girl will pay for this,' he said. 'I have been too nice to her.'

The little girl's mother and father
had heard the noise of the dogs
chasing after the bear, so they opened
their cottage door.

'What's this?' said her father when
he saw the basket. He opened the
basket and saw the cakes. Suddenly
they heard a little laugh. Then the
cakes began to move, and out jumped
their little girl.

The little girl told her mother and father
all about the big brown bear, his house
in the forest and the cakes she had made.
Then, with a smile, she told them how
she had got the bear to carry her all the
way home.

'What a clever little girl you are,' said her
mother and she gave her a big kiss.

Chapter 4

When the bear got home he was very
cross. He called up to the little girl
on the roof, 'Come down. Make my
dinner. I'm hungry.'
But nothing happened. So the bear
began to climb up on to the roof.

The bear climbed right up to the little girl and pulled off her hat. Next he pulled off her scarf and her coat and he saw that it was not the little girl at all. It was just a cross made of wood.

The bear let out a growl so loud that the little girl and her mother and father could hear it right across the forest. 'How stupid I have been!' said the bear. That little girl was too clever for me.'

From that day on, the little girl played near her cottage and she never, never went off into the forest again.

And as for the big brown bear ... he had to look after himself.